For my family, with love

First published in 2016 by Child's Play (International) Ltd
Ashworth Road, Bridgemead, Swindon SN5 7YD, UK

Published in USA by Child's Play Inc
250 Minot Avenue, Auburn, Maine 04210

Distributed in Australia by Child's Play Australia Pty Ltd
Unit 10/20 Narabang Way, Belrose, Sydney, NSW 2085

ISBN 978-1-84643-756-4
CLP141015CPL06167564

Printed in Shenzhen, China

1 3 5 7 9 10 8 6 4 2

A catalogue record of this book
is available from the British Library

www.childs-play.com

HOME and DRY

Sarah L Smith

Pitter-patter, pitter-patter, pours the rain.
A-whoosh! A-whoosh! howls the wind.
Drip, drip, drip, leaks the roof.
Creak, creak, creak, creaks the house.

Underneath this big, black rain cloud
is the home of Mrs Sally Paddling,
Mr Albert Paddling and their son.

Every morning, Sally Paddling wakes up
at six o'clock to catch fish for the day.

After breakfast, Albert Paddling and his son row upstream
to the nearby village, where Albert teaches swimming.

Every night, the rain goes
Pitter-patter, pitter-patter,
making the roof *Drip, drip, drip.*

And the wind goes
A-whoosh! A-whoosh!
making the house *Creak,
creak, creak,* and slowly
rocking everyone to sleep.

Every afternoon the local ferry people stop by.

They bring the Paddlings flour
and butter and sugar and milk.
They also bring
their mail.

This is how the Paddlings live most of the year,
but when summer comes along…

...the rain stops.   The cloud disappears.

The ferry people can't
bring food and mail.

Because, unfortunately
for the Paddlings...

...the sun comes out!

"Let's have a picnic further down," says Sally Paddling,
trying to be cheerful. "The water hasn't quite dried up over there."

Little do the Paddlings know, as they go in search of a place to paddle,
that *another* Mr Paddling would soon be arriving at their house.

Mr B Paddling, also known as Uncle Bastian, has worked all over the world for many years, living a lonely life in hotels and eating all by himself in restaurants.

A few days ago, he found a forgotten letter from his only nephew, who lived far away.

All of a sudden, he felt very sad that his life had passed by without Albert, who must now be grown up.

November 21st
Paddling View
On the Hill
Paddlington

Dear Uncle

How are you? We have not seen each other since I was very little! I hope one day soon you will be able to visit me and I can introduce you to my family.

With love
your nephew

Albert

So he wrote a letter.
"Dear Nephew Albert,
It has been too long
since I last saw you!
But when you receive
this letter…

I shall be on a train to Paddlington to visit you!"

And soon…

"Perfect," smiles Uncle Bastian.
"Thank you so much."

"Such a steep hill!" puffs Uncle Bastian.

Even though he waits...

and waits...

no one answers...

the door.

"No one is home!" cries Uncle Bastian.

As he starts walking back to the station,
the rain begins to fall: *Pitter-patter, pitter-patter*.

If only he knew the Paddlings
were just out paddling!

The water begins to rise higher and higher.

"Oh dear!"
says Sally Paddling.

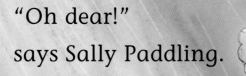

"Oh no!"
says Albert Paddling.

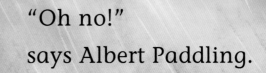

"Hurry! Hurry!"
think the children.

"Oh, help me! Anyone!"
cries Uncle Bastian hopelessly. "I can't swim."

Pitter-patter, pitter-patter.

A-whoosh! A-whoosh!

Poor Uncle Bastian is...

... saved, at last!

"I've got some mail for you, Mr Paddling!"
says the ferryman.
"For me?" asks Uncle Bastian.
"How do you know my name?"
"Oh no, it's for me," says Albert.
"I am Mr Paddling."

"But I am Mr Paddling too," replies a confused
Uncle Bastian, "and that letter is from me!"

"You must be my nephew, Albert!"

"I've come all this way to visit you!"

The rain is pouring, *Pitter-patter, pitter-patter,*
and the wind is howling, *A-whoosh! A-whoosh!*
The roof begins to leak again, *Drip, drip, drip,*
and the house begins to creak again, *Creak, creak, creak.*

Inside, Albert has cooked an enormous
fish supper for the family.

dinner is ready!

"Exquisite," declares Uncle Bastian.
"It's so good to be home and dry!"